A Witch In Time

VERONICA BLADE

Crush
PUBLISHING

Gardnerville, Nevada

A Witch in Time

Crush Publishing, Inc
Gardnerville, NV 89460

Crush Publishing, Inc name and logo are trademarks of Crush Publishing, Inc and are used only with its permission.

ISBN 978-0-9995994-5-7

Cover design and layout by Rose Nomura

Printed in the United States of America

For all my amazing readers

who have been so patient while I finished the Shapes of
Autumn series. Thank you for sticking with me!

♥

Chapter One

SLINGING THE STRAP of my laptop case over one shoulder, I dragged my carry-on toward Salt Lake City International Airport baggage claim. A restaurant window reflected my image and for the billionth time, I thanked my supernatural genes. I was in my seventies, but any human would assume I was in my late twenties to early thirties.

My thoughts drifted to Cedric, a vampire who had lived many centuries but who would never look older than me. Very soon, I'd see him again.

We'd met in California decades ago—ages before I had a child, long before I became queen to all witches, and an eternity before I married Boris, leader of the witch faction from whom I had eventually escaped.

I'd been just a girl then, an orphan looking for my place in the world and torn between two witch factions. Only months before I had turned eighteen, I had discovered I was a witch. I'd been on the run ever since, getting lost in crowds so both witch factions would have difficulty sensing me, not to mention other supernaturals.

One autumn evening after being cooped up too long, I donned a long-sleeved pink top and black slacks, then slipped into a pair of flats. After checking that my teased platinum-blond bouffant hadn't flattened, I abandoned my tiny motel room for a stroll. Once on Hollywood Boulevard, I immediately regretted it. Few people roamed the street. No crowds for me to hide in.

The last thing I had wanted to do was return to the room. My legs ached to stretch and, once on the sidewalk, I reveled in the fresh autumn air. I walked farther than I had intended and wished I had chosen tennis shoes in case I needed to run.

The aroma of syrup and sugar wafted toward me and I forged ahead toward the soda shop. An old dilapidated blue and white Buick cruised down my side of the street, slowed and then turned around to park across the road. Were those bullet holes on the fender?

Four gangsters hopped out of the car and sprinted my way, narrowly avoiding an oncoming car. Images from their minds rushed me, giving me insight into their nefarious intentions. As I quickened my pace, various ways to fend them off—without revealing myself as a witch—whirled through my head.

I hadn't seen much gang activity the last few times I had roamed Los Angeles, but I shouldn't have been surprised to see lawless activity so late at night.

A red-haired man with the greenest eyes I'd ever seen appeared out of nowhere. Perhaps if I hadn't been distracted by the hoodlums, I would've sensed him approaching. He intercepted the thugs, merely raising a palm, and they practically skidded to a halt. His impressive height, wide shoulders and confident attitude had them backing up without either of us touching them.

The scent of blood tickled my nose and I lifted my chin. Vampire.

They didn't scare me. But just to be on the safe side, I backed away.

The ginger inhaled, then squinted a moment as if realizing I was a witch. "Kind of late for you to be out on the streets alone."

Normally, gingers did nothing for me. And he wasn't the handsomest man I'd ever met. Still, he was very good-looking and I couldn't take my eyes off him. The confident manner in which he carried himself, the mischievous gleam in his green eyes and his beautiful grin drew me in.

But vampires were always charming—just before they sank their fangs into your flesh.

"I can take care of myself. I'd be happy to demonstrate if you'd like. If you need to feed, best try someone who can't remove your head with only her thoughts."

"I've already eaten, thank you. I was just on my way to grab some ice cream. How about joining me?" He hitched a thumb toward the soda shop about three stores up that I had been eyeing.

I raised a brow, my mouth refusing to return his smile. "No. Are you going to try to follow me home?"

"Probably not. I have to catch a plane in three hours." He thrust out a hand for me to take. "I'm Cedric."

Keeping my shield up and ready to shove him away with telekinesis, I cautiously shook his hand. "Cedric. Same name as the vampire king." Who I'd heard was a redhead.

His mouth curved up. "We share a name, yes."

In my peripheral vision, five men fanned out. Cedric noticed them too, nodded, and the men backed up. Must have been his guards. "I'll make sure they keep their distance."

My eyes narrowed as I crossed my arms over my chest. "How kind."

He laughed and spun. "I'll meet you at the soda shop," he threw over his shoulder. His men vanished into the background, between buildings and into doorways.

Planted in the same spot on the sidewalk, I watched Cedric slip through the door of the soda shop. I wanted to sit and talk with him. I'd been on the road for weeks and hadn't talked to many people. I'd engaged in light conversation in passing, sure. But I hadn't had a real conversation with another supernatural in months.

I'm in line. What should I order for you? he asked telepathically.

Witches couldn't talk telepathically. We could send and receive images, but no actual words. I would have to send him a picture of a root beer soda, but how would he know it wasn't regular cola?

Before I'd consciously decided to join him, my legs were already moving. A flicker in the corner of my eye told me Cedric's guards were on alert. I'd never met a vampire who had guards.

I halted just before the cafe door and blinked. Kings had guards. Cedric didn't just have the same name as the vampire king. This Cedric was the king himself. How much danger would I put myself in by spending any more time with him?

But if I stayed on guard and didn't screw up, could they really hurt me? Vampires *and* werewolves were stronger than witches, but we had powers they couldn't get past.

From what I had heard of King Cedric Gallagher, he was ancient and powerful. I'd also heard of his benevolence, and how he strived for peace among all supernatural species.

I swung the shop door open and crossed the threshold, immediately spotting Cedric in line. Elvis blared from the speakers as I sidled up next to him. "Even kings have to wait in line, huh?"

One side of his mouth curled up. "And even kings need good conversation."

"Root beer, please." I grinned and pointed at a table in the corner near the window. "That spot okay?"

"Yes. You'll want your back to the wall, of course, so you can watch my friends." He swiveled toward the cashier and gave our orders.

And that was precisely why I had wanted that particular table. I made my way to it, claiming the seat against the wall. While keeping Cedric on my radar, I scanned for his guards, locating all of them. Fortunately, the shop was nearly empty. A young man and woman chatted at a table near the opposite end of the room and that was it. Good. Fewer people for me to have to watch.

"This place has the best ice cream." He sat a glass in front of me filled with caramel liquid and ice floating on the top. He handed me a long spoon and dipped his own spoon into the oval dish filled with vanilla ice cream and topped with chocolate syrup. "I come here as often as I can. The palace can get stuffy. Sometimes, I just want to meet new people."

Exactly my reason for leaving the motel room. I leaned across the table and scooped up a small bite of ice cream. Then we chatted about everything from dogs to movies. As the moments passed, I relaxed. I lost track of time and eventually the shop brightened when all the lights were turned up. Our cue to leave.

Cedric stood, holding out his hand for me. "They're closing."

Sadness blanketed me. I didn't want to leave. I could've talked to him for weeks or months. Or a lifetime. He left a few bills on the table and then he opened the door for me. Once outside, I paused, not wanting to say goodbye.

"You can't run forever," he whispered, playing with a lock of my platinum blond hair. "At some point, and it won't be long, they'll find you. And then it might be too late to choose."

I straightened my shoulders, knowing I'd made the best decision I could. "I already chose. I ran."

Cedric gave me sad smile and shook his head. "You know it doesn't work like that. You have to choose sides. If you don't, then both sides hunt you. It's only a matter of time before they find you."

My chin quivered. "I don't know which side to pick. I'm afraid that if I choose badly, I'll end up dead."

"Choose the strongest side. Convince them you're loyal. Be smart. Be patient. Then make your plans to leave. For instance... you could fake your death. Until then, you can never be truly free of them." He reached into his pocket and pulled out a card. "If I can help with anything, scheming or whatnot, I hope you won't hesitate to call me."

I offered him a shy smile, knowing I was way too young for a centuries-old man. And as the vampire king, he wouldn't waste his time on an eighteen-year-old witch when he could have just about any woman he wanted. I had no business being infatuated with him.

Proving he had no feeling for me beyond friendship— and possibly empathy—he leaned forward and dropped a kiss on the top of my head. "Stay well, little witch."

I didn't want him to go. I didn't want to go back to my motel room either. What I really wanted was to ask him to take me with him. Loneliness had driven me out of my motel room, but as I watched him cross the street to reunite with his guards, I'd never felt lonelier in my life.

Chapter Two

THE BAGGAGE CLAIM sign loomed ahead and I slowed my pace, my stomach twisting and churning as I remembered that evening with Cedric long ago. Decades later and I was still hideously infatuated with the handsome ginger man. Well, he was still many centuries older than me and next to him, I was still a child. Our difference in species hadn't changed, except now I had my own kingdom to rule. He wouldn't desert his people and settle several hundred miles away any more than I would.

I stopped alongside the wall of the endless corridor and rolled my shoulders. Why was I getting so worked up? I had called Cedric several times over the decades for advice: first to plan my fake death and later when I became queen to occasionally seek his counsel in ruling my people. And all those times, he never once asked me to meet him again, didn't try to woo me to a deserted island where no one knew who we were. He just wasn't interested.

Cedric was a king and didn't pick people up at airports. He would probably send a car, but he wasn't hosting this supernatural peace summit, nor was Salt

Lake City his home. Autumn, the werewolf queen, would send a driver or a servant.

Whoever came for me, I shouldn't keep them waiting. After rearranging the heavy laptop bag, I straightened and forged toward the sign. After barely progressing three feet, I froze. People milled about in all directions, rushing to someone they'd just spotted or grabbing their luggage off the conveyor belt. Standing still as a vampire, a tall ginger-haired man's green eyes watched me from just under the baggage claim sign.

He flashed me a big, beautiful grin and my heart skipped a beat. He sprinted to me, stopping about a foot away. "Hello, little witch."

My laptop slid off my shoulders, my fingers lost their grip on the handle of my luggage, and I leaped up. My arms wrapped around his neck and I held on for dear life. "Cedric!"

His arms circled me and squeezed, pressing me against him. I knew I had to release him soon or my crush on him would be painfully obvious, so I relaxed my hold. But he didn't fully let me go and I slid down slowly, feeling the length of his body against mine.

Focus. I was a queen and grandmother, for crying out loud. Too old to be thrown by a handsome face and sexy smile. But I would never act aloof. Not with Cedric. We were true friends and for all the help he'd given me over the years, he deserved my respect. "So good to see you again."

"You look incredible. Exactly the same, except all grown up." His gaze swept the length of me.

"Thank you." My face warmed. To cover his effect on me, I reached down for my laptop. "I guess we should get out of everyone's way."

Cedric gently slipped the strap of the laptop case from my fingers and threw it over his shoulder. Then he took the carry-on. "I'll hang on to these. Get your luggage."

While I searched for my suitcase, I snuck peeks at Cedric. He was scanning the area, his brows furrowed in irritation. Seeing my suitcase, I plucked it off the conveyor belt and rolled it toward Cedric.

"Where are your guards?" His green eyes bored through me, narrowing when I didn't answer him. "You didn't bring any guards, did you?"

I scoffed. "I'm the most powerful witch on the planet. I don't need guards."

Cedric growled and turned on his heel toward the exit. In my peripheral vision, a man and a woman shadowed Cedric. He indicated for them to follow, which they would've done anyway.

Why did I always feel like a child around Cedric? He had no right to be angry with me if I chose not to have guards. I had plenty of other things for my staff to do than waste precious time on something unnecessary. Sprinting to keep up with his long strides, I slowed when we reached a white limousine.

A vampire in a black suit and cap stepped forward and relieved Cedric of my things, stowing them in the trunk. "I'm Jane," I told the driver.

"I'm Joseph, Your Majesty—driver and security at your service," he said, arranging my carry-on next to my suitcase.

"Very nice to meet you." I swiveled toward the other two vampires, another man and the gorgeous black woman. "Thank you for escorting me." Even though I didn't need protection.

"I'm Kayla and this is Tony." The black woman offered a warm smile as she hitched a thumb at the tall dark guard. He nodded and they hovered until the driver closed the hood.

I trailed after Cedric, who was climbing into the limo, then I claimed the seat on the opposite side with my back to the driver.

The limo moved, then stopped, and I shifted forward, then backward again. I repositioned myself, stretching out a leg for balance so I wouldn't lurch toward Cedric every time the limo accelerated.

"Drink?" He reached into a compartment at his side and offered me a bottle of water.

"Yes, thank you." I grabbed the bottle, my fingertips grazing his, and quickly sunk back into my seat.

"About your guards..." Cedric tilted his head. "This is a pivotal meeting of great importance, and there are those who wish for us to fail. Anything could have happened to you."

"Cedric, I'm perfectly capable of handling myself. You know that."

"Your pride, your courage and tenacity, not to mention your stubbornness, are what I admire most about you. But there is a time and place for everything. You're in an unfamiliar city and the enemy could strike at any moment. I doubt King Zack and Queen Autumn can spare any of their men to guard you, not with all their extra guests this week. I have people with me and they can protect both of us. You'll go nowhere without me. Understand?"

Stay with Cedric twenty-four hours a day? Didn't seem like a bad deal. Except that I was already smitten and didn't need to fall for him any more than I already had.

On the other hand, how well did I really know Cedric? An evening at a soda shop many decades ago, and occasional snatches of conversation by phone didn't give me in-depth knowledge of him. Maybe if we spent more time together and I got to know him, my infatuation would subside. If not, then I'd certainly get drunk on him, wouldn't I? Seemed like a win-win bargain to me.

"Cedric, I don't need guards. But if it makes you feel better, thank you for your generous offer. I accept." The limo turned and I swayed to the side. "Tell me about your kingdom. Who's ruling in your stead? Your second in command, Dathan?"

"Actually, I'm *his* second in command. He's still here at the werewolf castle—about to be married, actually. If you had arrived tomorrow, you would have missed it. I hope you like weddings." He grinned.

"Right. I'd heard about him and the shape-shifter queen. If she's in northern Nevada and he rules from southern California, how is that going to work? I guess he's sticking you with the job a little longer?" If Dathan never took his rightful place on the throne, Cedric would always be ruling on his behalf. All the more reason I could never be with Cedric. I had my own kingdom to run.

Why did I keep talking myself out of being with Cedric? Being with him wasn't possible anyway. He clearly wasn't interested, as he'd demonstrated over the years. It was a nonissue.

"Actually, her son will be taking over for her. She'll be joining Dathan at the vampire palace." Cedric shrugged, giving me a lopsided smile. "And I'll be out of a job."

I laughed. "You don't seem too broken up about it. What are you going to do?"

"I haven't decided yet." He scratched his chin, lost in thought. "I haven't traveled much this last century. I'll probably go abroad, see how the world has changed."

I squashed any hope that he'd consider visiting me in Scottsdale, reminding myself that he had never seen me as anything other than the "little witch."

"When is the ceremony?" I removed the cap from the bottle and took a swig of water.

"This evening. They'll stay here until the summit is over, then they'll go straight onto their honeymoon. So I'll be king for a little while longer." He watched me, his green eyes bright with mischief. "What about you? Giving up your throne anytime soon? A vacation perhaps? You've earned some time to yourself."

Was he hinting at me to go with him? Of course not. That was just my foolish heart's wishful thinking. "Maybe one day. Right now, I just want to see how the summit goes. I can't imagine all the splinter groups and rogues suddenly toeing the line just because the leaders agree on peace. We'll always be in danger. I'm not sure traveling for any length of time is a smart idea."

Cedric snorted. "Says the woman who didn't bring any bodyguards with her."

He had me there. I cleared my throat. "Touché. Truth be told, I've always viewed giving up my independence as a loss of power. If I need guards, that means I'm weak."

He dropped his bottle in the cup holder, planted his elbows on his knees and bent toward me. "I just want you safe."

My chest tingled and I reminded myself to lighten things up. I couldn't take his words in a romantic way. I pasted on a grin. "Then it's a good thing I'm under your protection."

Cedric leaned back again, the corners of his mouth lifting. "I'm glad you're here. It's been too long."

Why did he always seem to have a deeper meaning to every word out of his mouth? I needed to pull myself together and stop imagining the impossible. My phone vibrated and I was relieved not to be obligated to respond to him. I fished in my purse for my cell and glanced at the screen. "Excuse me a moment."

Did you arrive safely? my granddaughter Tessa texted.

Cedric had really thrown me if I hadn't even remembered to let my family know I had arrived. *Landed safe and on my way to the werewolf castle. Love you.*

I didn't think my nerves could take a full week of around-the-clock with Cedric. Why had I given in to Queen Autumn's insistence that I arrive several days earlier than the summit? Yes, she was grateful for the witches' help in overthrowing the previous werewolf regime and she wanted to show her appreciation. But why the rush?

In the end, I had booked the soonest available flight. Good relations helped both sides and bonding with the new werewolf rulers was a smart move for witches all around the world. My species' survival was my number one priority. But by attending this summit and working toward my people's future, I was endangering my own stability. After a week with Cedric, would I ever be the same? Or would I only be more aware of what was missing in my life?

Chapter Three

CEDRIC HAD INSISTED I sit next to him during the ceremony. We had an agreement that I was under his protection, after all. We sat on the groom's side near the front, with Kayla, Tony and Joseph watching from the background.

I hadn't expected the ceremony to be held on the grounds of the werewolf palace. My stilettos had sunk into the grass with each step. Cedric provided an arm at all times to steady me if my heels dug in too deep. Fortunately, with superhuman strength came superhuman balance so I didn't need the arm. But I took it anyway. I could admit, at least to myself, I liked the feel of his muscular arms.

The air smelled of freshly mowed grass and despite its short height, it was lush and green. Fall temperatures cooled in the early evening, making the weather perfect. Twinkle lights lit up the trees and layers of sheer fabric covered the gazebo. Stunning flower arrangements of white and pink filled every view.

"Why aren't you Dathan's best man?" I whispered to Cedric. "Doesn't he like you?"

Cedric chuckled. "I got dumped for his future stepson. Benjamin was imprisoned for a century and only freed weeks ago when they overthrew Mortimer. Dathan wants him to have every chance to meet people. Exposure is good, especially since he'll be taking Natasha's place on the throne."

"Being bumped doesn't bother you?" I scrunched up my nose.

He lifted a casual shoulder. "If I was up there by Dathan's side, I wouldn't be right here with you."

I swallowed, not knowing what to say. And, damn, what did that even mean? The music started, saving me from a reply. When I turned from Cedric to watch the bride walk down the aisle, I recognized Natasha's brother Eli escorting her. She radiated happiness and her blond hair cascaded in luxurious curls around her bare shoulders and lace straps. The white gown hugged her tiny waist, molded to her hips and flared midthigh.

Natasha gazed ahead, but as she neared the gazebo, her gaze met mine. "Thank you," she mouthed.

My heart warmed. "You're welcome," I mouthed back.

I wasn't sure if I could handle any more gratitude. And, honestly, when Dathan and the shifters had originally asked for help, I had refused to allow any of my witches to go into battle. The only reason my granddaughters defied me was because one of them, Zoe, had decided to rebel against me.

Zoe had been physically weak and mentally fragile since we'd rescued her from being buried alive. Ten years in a coffin with only herself for company left an awful lot of playtime for demons. So I provided her with peace and calm, sheltering her from anything that might throw her into a spin. Instead of appreciating my efforts to keep her safe and happy, she accused me of hovering and insisted she needed freedom to do something meaningful. With or without my blessing, she would go into battle.

Sending my other granddaughter Tessa and their two guards had increased my chance of getting them all back in one piece. But my girls didn't do all the hard work in overthrowing the werewolf king and they couldn't have triumphed by themselves. That didn't stop the werewolves and shape-shifters from giving me credit, even though I hadn't lifted a finger to help.

Sighing, I vowed to get my mind off my wayward granddaughters and over-appreciative supernaturals and enjoy the wedding—and Cedric's company. But not too much.

Dathan and Natasha kept their vows short enough to leave me wanting more. As we moved toward the reception area inside the mansion, I thought about how I hadn't been with a man since I'd escaped from Boris and faked my death over a decade ago. For years, I had stayed in hiding, and then I took control of the faction opposing Boris. All my energy had gone toward building my empire, while keeping everyone I loved safe. Those tasks had left little time for men. I could admit, at least to myself, that since my species had found peace, and my family was safe, I'd been pining to find love.

And Cedric had spent way too much time in my head over the years.

My gaze strayed to the doorway. A werewolf woman hovered at the entryway, her eyes darting around the room, finally landing on Hannah, Queen Autumn's mother. Hannah was slow-dancing with her husband Eli, each lost in each other.

"Excuse me a moment," I whispered to Cedric, who was talking to Renzo, King Zack's dad. I felt like a bit of a third wheel anyway. I strolled to the woman and held out my hand in greeting. "I'm Jane. Can I help you?"

"I didn't realize I'd be interrupting a wedding today." She licked her lips nervously. "Who is getting married, may I ask?"

If she hadn't come for the wedding, how had she gotten past the guards? "Dathan the vampire king and Natasha the shaper-shifter queen." My mouth quirked. "Nothing surprises me anymore."

"Natasha, formerly known as Isabella," she whispered. "Sister to the legendary Eli who escaped with the king's betrothed Hannah?"

"Yes, I believe that's how the story goes." I scanned the room for Dathan and Natasha who were nowhere to be seen. This woman seemed nice enough, but I wasn't taking any chances. I sent a mental picture of her to Cedric. Having backup never hurt. "How did you get in?"

"One of them recognized me from a long time ago." She offered a hesitant smile.

Judging by the power emanating from her, it was a *very* long time ago. She was obviously ancient. "I'll take you to Hannah."

She nodded and walked alongside me as we

approached Hannah, who was walking off the dance floor, hands joined with Eli. Just a few feet away, Hannah froze as if sensing something, then slowly turned toward us. After a sharp intake of breath, she sprinted toward the woman. I wasn't sure if that was good or bad.

"Mrs. Benton!" Hannah hugged her tightly and it went on for what seemed like minutes. I didn't want to intrude on their reunion, but now I was intrigued. "I thought you'd been killed. After Mortimer was slain, I tried reaching you and got nothing. I can't tell you how happy I am to see you. I've missed you so much."

Tears dribbled down Mrs. Benton's face. "You know me, loyal to a fault. I wanted to stay with Mortimer and my people to help the newcomers as best I could. But about a hundred years ago, he became too unstable. I followed your lead and escaped through the tunnels. Your recent calls didn't reach me because I was on another continent. I've moved around a lot so Mortimer's men couldn't find me, and stayed far enough away that he couldn't easily sense me. I didn't hear word of the kinder management until a week ago and I got here as soon as I could."

"They didn't find you because they were too busy hunting Eli and me." At last, Hannah released Mrs. Benton and turned to me. "Mrs. Benton and I knew each other centuries ago. In fact, she was more of a mother to me than my own mother. Later, she helped me escape King Mortimer."

"I only showed you a tunnel. You and Eli did the rest." Mrs. Benton's red mop of hair swished around her shoulders in denial as she shook her head.

"I hope you enjoy your stay," I interrupted, my curiosity satisfied. "It was nice meeting you."

"Same to you." Mrs. Benton squeezed my hand. "I'll see you again."

"Mrs. Benton, I think it's about time you meet my daughter." Hannah beamed and dragged her away.

Although I probably should've mingled and visited with others, I returned to Cedric. Circling around and networking with the leaders and elites who filled the hall could only help me. But all I really wanted to do was spend time with Cedric. A grin waited for me as soon as he spotted me making a beeline for him. I'd made the right decision.

Or was it the wrong decision? Whatever. I intended to enjoy him as long as I was in Utah. My return flight to Scottsdale, Arizona would come soon enough.

"Dance?" Cedric asked, as soon as I rejoined him.

Absolutely not. He had quite an effect on me without even touching me. I didn't want to imagine the puddle— or stuttering fool—I'd become if his fingertips made contact with my lower back or if he pressed me against him. If he swayed to the music and moved against me, I'd probably faint.

"I'd love to, but no. I'm just enjoying watching everyone else. Thank you, though." I smiled so he wouldn't feel rejected.

"Queen Jane." Autumn strode toward me. "Now that all the social obligations are done, I want to steal you away for a private chat."

"Oh?" I couldn't fathom what on earth she wanted to talk privately about. "Are we starting the summit early?"

"Nope. Just the two of us. There's a reason I urged you to come early. Follow me." Autumn wrapped her hand around mine and led me inside the mansion and down a hallway.

"She's not getting out of my sight," Cedric told Autumn and caught up with us.

I twisted, laid a hand on his chest and instantly regretted the physical contact when butterflies battled in my stomach. "I'm sure I'll be perfectly safe with Autumn."

Cedric's head whipped side-to-side. "I don't see any guards around. Do you? I'm all you've got."

"Actually…" Autumn nodded. "You can come, if she doesn't mind. We're all a part of this."

How could that be? "What is this about?"

"You'll see." Autumn rocketed out of the great hall and into the corridor.

Picking up my pace, I shot Cedric a questioning look. He shrugged. We stopped at a metal door and she punched in a code, then descended the short set of stairs.

"This used to be the dungeon, but it's being converted to staff quarters. Zack insisted on doing most of the cleanup and repairs, because he didn't want the others to be reminded of what happened here. When he was going through his old things in the closet where he slept, he discovered something very interesting." After a couple more turns, she stopped and entered a closet, then waved us in.

"We're all going to fit in there?" I asked, not wanting to be that close to Cedric.

"Plenty of room in the tunnels." Autumn pulled out the shelves and set them aside. Then she wedged her fingers into the corner, pushed and removed the panel. "Zack set up lights so we can read easily. Cedric, would you close the door, please? I'm not sure I want to call attention to us being here, at least not until Jane has seen what we found."

This little adventure was getting stranger. I bent lower so my head would clear the passageway to the tunnel then straightened once through. Lights had been set up and someone had brought in chairs, blocking the rest of the tunnel. "You made yourself comfortable, I see."

"We've spent some time in here." Autumn reached up to a ledge near the ceiling. After blindly feeling around, she pulled down an old leather-bound book that appeared to be a journal of sorts. She stacked one after the other on her free arm while retrieving more. "I've been so busy preparing for the wedding, I didn't make a note which one has the information."

"Can I help?" Cedric asked.

"I got them." She sat on one of the chairs, balancing the stack of journals on her lap, then picked up one at a time and flipped through the pages. About halfway through the third journal, she flicked the page. "Queen Jane, brace yourself."

Cedric's brows rose as we exchanged glances. "I don't understand," I said.

She popped up, her hands clamped to the journal against her chest, her finger holding the spot where she'd stopped reading. "When we were at your place in Scottsdale, Zoe said something about being buried alive." She cleared her throat. "And then I remembered Dathan mentioning this woman, Rebecca, who he suspected was your mother."

My breath caught and I steeled myself from getting my hopes up. She couldn't be alive but I'd always wanted to know where I had come from. "Is that journal about her?"

"Yes." She held the book tighter as if I might pluck it from her arms. "I spoke with Dathan and he said I should get you here immediately. Because divine witches—that's you and your granddaughters—aren't killed as easily as other witches."

And my mother wouldn't be killed as easily as other witches either. Was she alive somewhere and suffering as Zoe had? "Can I read that?"

"Absolutely. You should see for yourself what Mortimer wrote." Autumn handed me the journal, opening it to the page I needed to read.

After scanning a few passages, nausea rose up and I stumbled back. "Oh, my god."

Cedric caught me, pulled me close and stroked my hair. "You think her mother is still alive after all this time?" he asked Autumn.

"That is a definite possibility," she answered.

I shook my head, still struggling not to vomit. My mother had disappeared when I was a baby. Over seventy years ago. If she'd been buried and alone all this time...

I couldn't think about it, couldn't go there at all.

I disengaged from Cedric and bolted through the small door and into the closet, then flung open the door. In the dungeon hallway, I sucked in a lungful of air and wiped the tears from my eyes.

When we'd found Zoe after being buried for ten years, she was a different girl than the one I'd known before she'd "died." She'd been fragile of both mind and body for years, up until Dathan and the shifters had arrived and asked for our help in battle. The mission and everything it meant for all species had pulled Zoe out of the hell she'd plummeted into, and the higher purpose had healed her damaged soul.

That had been only ten years of mental prison, of being alone and trapped with only her own demons for company. How would my mother fare after seventy long years? If I found her and she was still alive, even after she healed, would she be capable of any kind of quality of life?

Cedric's strong arms wrapped around me. "I'll stay with you, whatever your decision."

I rested my head on his shoulder, soaking in his soothing calm. After a moment, I lifted my chin to see his face. "I have a decision to make?" No, no, no. I didn't want to think about my mother's horror, much less make any choices.

"Yes. You have new information on Rebecca," Cedric said. "What are you going to do about it?"

Autumn appeared in the corridor. "It shouldn't be too difficult. The journal details where he lived seventy years ago, and where he put her." She tilted her head, tapping her chin. "I don't know if Mrs. Benton is familiar with that particular building, but she worked with Mortimer for centuries. She understood him and how he worked. Maybe she can help." Autumn paused and softened her voice. "Unless you'd rather leave everyone else out of this."

I squeezed my eyes shut while I sorted through my thoughts. First, I could never forget what I now knew. Second, I couldn't leave anyone alive and trapped forever, mother or not. "I would appreciate Mrs. Benton's help. But I need to leave right away. *If* Rebecca really was a divine witch and buried alive all this time, I can't let her suffer one second longer."

Autumn stroked my arm. "I anticipated that. Which is why I asked the servants to leave your belongings alone. Figured you'd appreciate not having to pack all over again. I'm only sorry I had to fulfill other obligations today. If I could have put off my aunt and uncle's wedding, I would have."

"It's fine." I glanced at the journal in my hand, so thankful for its existence. "Of course you can't plan your life around mine and you couldn't have known you'd find Mortimer's journals. Perhaps you could arrange for someone to drop me off at a car rental place?"

"No way." Autumn shook her head. "You can use one of ours. It's the least we can do."

"You're not going alone," Cedric told me, then switched to Autumn. "Where are we going?"

"Before I tell you"—Autumn hesitated a moment— "your given name couldn't be Jane Doe. I'm just dying to know your real name."

"Me too, actually. I was never sure if what the orphanage called me was my real name or not. When I ran away and didn't want to be found, I picked Jane Doe because I liked the anonymity it gave me."

"Now I'm intrigued." Cedric sidled up next to me. "What did the orphanage call you?"

Autumn had taken care to share the journal with me and possibly reunite me with my mother. I should share my secret with her. "Jade Vance. Jade was similar enough to Jane, so..."

Silence filled the dungeon corridor for a moment, then Autumn gently squeezed my arm. "I'll go arrange your transportation and speak with Mrs. Benton." She jogged down the hallway and around the corner. A few seconds later, the door clicked shut.

I didn't want to read any more of the journal. But I needed to. My fingertips tapped the book in my hand.

"Do you want to be alone while you continue reading it?"

I wrinkled my nose. "Not really. I don't want to come across like a big baby, but would you stay with me?"

"Of course," he said and leaned against the opposite wall, as if to give me some space.

I scanned the section in the book where I'd left off. After reading every word on the page, my stomach churned again and my fingers trembled. "He'd tried to kill her once before and she didn't die. He thought it was a fluke. So he killed her again by stabbing her until she'd bled out, then he locked her away in a dungeon and sealed it completely so she would run out of air, believing that if she wasn't already dead, she would be soon."

Cedric groaned. "He thought she was a regular witch and would die like one. But your kind can only be killed the same as my kind, decapitation or dismemberment and burned to ashes. She's alive."

"After seventy years, I'm not sure anyone would view her condition as being alive." I sighed. "But she's not dead."

"Where is she?" Cedric asked, stepping forward and grazing my wrists with his fingertips.

"Granger, Wyoming." Wherever that was.

Cedric nodded. "Yes, I remember. Mortimer stayed at that castle, if anyone would call it that, for about two centuries before leaving about seventy years ago. Let's go."

Feeling a little disoriented, I let him steer me out of the dungeon and back to the great hall. "Wait here," he said, after maneuvering me to a chair. "I'll be right back."

The party was in full swing and guilt filled me for monopolizing Cedric when he should be mingling. I scanned the guests who danced, ate and laughed, wishing I could be carefree like them.

"Queen Jane?" Mrs. Benton loomed before me and I stood. "I can take you to the old castle in Granger."

"No, I don't want you to leave. You just reunited with Hannah. You should stay here."

"Call me Charlotte, and I'm going. I know that castle. I lived there for more than a century before escaping." She flashed me a grin. "Besides, Hannah's coming too. And Eli. We'll be able to catch up on the way there."

I didn't want everyone putting themselves out for

me. But I needed them. The bigger the search party, the faster we'd find Rebecca. "Thank you so much."

Hannah joined us, a car key dangling from her fingers. "Autumn is giving us use of the Discovery. We'll be ready to leave in ten minutes."

"We'll follow you in my Bentley." Cedric glanced at me for confirmation and I nodded. "Five of us, plus a couple guards still gives us room for Rebecca. Once we find her, you guys could be free to leave."

Cedric and I split up, each going to our own room to collect our things. Since I suspected I might have to do some dirty work or trek through hills, I changed into a pair of jeans, a lightweight long-sleeved shirt and hiking boots, then I gathered my hair into a ponytail. Now was not the time for vanity. Leaving my laptop on the bed, I grabbed my jacket. October brought chilly nights.

Granger was only two hours away, but I had no idea what it would be like once we got there or how long before we found Rebecca. I loaded my carry-on into the back of the SUV. Cedric arrived and tossed his own duffel bag in with mine.

Two of his guards, Kayla and Joseph, showed up with blankets, a tool bag and two shovels, then squeezed all of it in the back, along with their own small bags. "Mind if I drive?" Cedric asked me, glancing at his two guards. They quickly climbed into the second seat.

"Please." My anxiety over where Rebecca might be hidden, how we would get to her and how long before we could revive her would distract me too much to pay proper attention to the road.

I climbed into the front passenger side of the Bentley Bentayga and Cedric steered the SUV down the long driveway of the werewolf castle.

His guards didn't seem very talkative and I couldn't imagine Cedric going beyond idle chitchat, if at all, with an audience. I would have lots of time to think. That was for the best. I couldn't let Cedric worm his way any further into my heart. That was reserved for my own species, who had earned my undying love and loyalty. I doubted I could ever get that from a different species and I could never settle for less.

For now, my focus needed to be on Rebecca.

Chapter Four

WE ENTERED GRANGER just a little over two hours later. The pearl black Land Rover Discovery ahead of us cruised slowly, navigating over the dirt road with only the headlights to guide us. Though we all had better vision than humans, the pitch-black outside still challenged us.

Adrenaline roared through my body in my anxiety to get to the old castle and start looking for my mom. If Rebecca was my biological mother. Hell, maybe she wasn't even a divine witch. Maybe she wasn't here at all.

Cedric swerved the SUV to avoid a hole in the road, the tire hitting the edge of the crater and dipping. "Hannah just talked to me, says Charlotte is looking for the spot where the building used to be. She remembers it being hidden behind a hill and trees. But she assumes he blew the place up when he left, as usual. Since this particular castle was mostly underground, might be tricky to find."

"Lovely. Sealed in a tomb, air cut off and the place blown up. If she's alive, she's probably in pieces." My chest squeezed. I didn't want to admit how badly I wanted to meet my mother.

The Land Rover turned around a hill and disappeared. A moment later, Cedric parked his white Bentley Bentayga behind it. Hannah, Eli and Charlotte had climbed out ahead of us, already scanning the area. I darted out of the Bentley and caught up to the werewolves, knowing Cedric and the other vampires could take care of themselves.

"This is it?" Under the years of dirt, I could just make out chunks of broken stone and slabs of splintered wood. "We were supposed to find a castle."

"Mortimer demolished every place we left." Charlotte stomped on the ground, listening for different sounds and echoes. "With this particular building, he wanted to blend into the terrain and much of the living space was built underground. When it exploded, I imagine it just fell into itself, which is why we don't see much from the surface. I just have to find an entry point."

"She was thrown into the far end of a dungeon and then they bricked around her. How will we know where she is?" I asked.

Charlotte's eyes searched every tree and every boulder. "Give me a moment while I compare my memory to what I see now."

Joseph and Kayla passed out flashlights. After a quick search, Charlotte pointed at a spot with a pile of broken wood beams, part of a collapsed roof and a scattering of tin cans and metal chunks.

Cedric slung an arm around my shoulder when I shivered. "She's doing the best she can. And if we have to, we'll get a crew out here to excavate."

But I didn't want to waste anymore time. Rebecca needed to be free now. She'd suffered enough.

Charlotte stared at the collapsed roof, tapping her chin. She spun and headed further out, then halted between a huge rock and a mound. "I need more light." Each of our flashlights flooded the area into brightness and Charlotte squeezed past some brush, then stomped her foot again. That was wood and it sounded hollow. An opening. "I think this is the access."

My breath caught and I rushed to the spot. "A hatch?"

"When you mentioned her being thrown into the farthest end of the dungeon, I remembered that Mortimer always made sure there were plenty of ways in and out of any building he occupied. We all know how he liked his secret passages." Charlotte knelt and swept away dirt with her palms. "If the building didn't come with tunnels, he'd have his workers make them. And he never took the time to make sure every inch of the structure was destroyed—too time-consuming. He usually just leveled the main portion."

After digging her fingers into the edges of the wood, Charlotte stepped aside and lifted the hatch, then swung the cover over.

I aimed the light down. "The interior appears intact." And only about eight feet deep. I jumped, landing on the stone floor. After glancing up, I hoped I could get back out. The rickety ladder against the wall appeared to be hundreds of years old and, judging by the rough surface, termites had fed well.

Spider webs hung low, and something small and

furry scampered off. Locating a long piece of wood, I used it to move aside the cobwebs. Someone landed behind me, but I kept going. The metallic scent told me the new arrival was Cedric. Another thump told me a third person had taken the leap, and then two more.

"I remember this place." Charlotte ran her hands along a cement wall. "I think she's in here."

Cedric examined the connecting wall, searching for a crevice or a way through. "We need to be careful. If Rebecca is on the other side of the wall, her body is desiccated and weakened. Muscles and ligaments that normally connect parts of her body could be compromised. We can't risk breaking her in any way."

"Over here," Hannah said from the other end of the wall. "Loose stone. I think I can remove it."

Cedric returned to the spot where we'd entered and landed. "Joseph, Kayla, can one of you send down the bag of tools?" he shouted into the hole above.

Gratitude filled me that Cedric had thought of everything. Joseph dropped the tool bag and Cedric caught it. He darted back to Hannah, and I stood uselessly while they hammered and picked their way through the wall, stone by stone.

"Are you sure you don't want me to do that?" I asked, anxious to be of value, especially since they were all doing this for *me*. I didn't want to put them out any more than I had. "I'm perfectly capable."

"This gives me something to do," Cedric replied, repositioning a pick, then tapping it with the hammer. "We got this. You'll need your energy when we find her."

Eli shot me a sympathetic look. "I'm feeling rather impotent at the moment watching my wife get dirt under her fingernails. But she's already shoved me away once."

Hannah chuckled, then her smile faded as she rose to study the wall. "I sense a presence. Not vampire. Not werewolf or shape-shifter."

Why hadn't I thought to telepathically search for Rebecca? I crowded around the wall they were dismantling, closed my eyes and sent out my mental tentacles. A thrill ran through me when I felt someone behind the wall—which meant that person was alive. The opening was about two feet in diameter now. "Someone's definitely in there. I'd like to shine the light inside."

Cedric scooted aside to make room for me. My pulse pounded wildly as I aimed the light through the hole. I started at the left and slowly moved the beam, studying every shape and shadow.

A thin human-shaped lump lay curled up in the fetal position, hands joined under her chin, blond hair spiking from her emaciated skull. Her clothes were tattered and I wondered if they would stay intact as her body healed and shifted position. "I see her."

Sticking the flashlight in farther, I set it down, then squeezed through the opening. I didn't want to risk the tomb collapsing around me as we dismantled the connecting wall, so I pushed one wall, then stretched up to the ceiling and pressed a palm into the stone above. "Seems solid enough. Give me an axe or hammer or something and I'll work on it from inside. I'll need enough room to move her out without damaging her."

"You shouldn't move her anytime soon," Cedric said, handing me a hammer. "She'll have to rehydrate. Fortunately, when the moisture leaves the body, it also hardens. On the other hand, bone is hard too, and it breaks. Also, after so long without sustenance, the body is prone to bruising, even if you and I don't notice it."

"How do you know so much about desiccated supernaturals?" I eyed the wall before heaving the hammer at a stone nearest the opening. Chunks dropped and I kicked them out of the way.

"Vampire hunters often assume that a stake in the heart kills us. I've been reviving vampires since I was a newbie."

What happened to vampires who were left in the elements where animals could find them? Relief filled me that Rebecca had been sealed in the tomb where harmful elements were limited.

How on earth would I get her out of there? I didn't even know how long it would take to revive her or how that would be done. I paused my assault on the wall and poked my head out of my mother's cell to see Cedric. "But we can move her soon, right?"

He nodded. "In a little while, yes, but for now we have to be careful. We don't want her body expending any extra energy repairing damage we did."

"Okay." Focus. One stone block at a time. I returned to my task, slamming the hammer on another stone at the opening until it crumbled, the hole widening. On the other side of the wall, Hannah removed another section, the hole expanding more.

"I'm coming through." Cedric stuffed a pick in his pocket, ducked and squeezed inside, immediately locating Rebecca.

"You think she hears us?" I asked.

He set his flashlight on the ground, positioned it at the opening and shook his head. "The brain petrifies and becomes unusable. For a supernatural, that's equivalent to a coma."

I squeezed my eyes shut and sagged. "Thank God. I was imagining the worst, that she'd been trapped in her own mind all this time, unable to see or move."

"A decade or so of suffering maybe. After that, she'd drift off into a deeper and deeper sleep. A welcome oblivion, I'm sure." Cedric scratched his jaw. "Unless after bleeding out, she remained unconscious and never woke because she couldn't heal."

I hoped that was how it happened. After loosening two more hunks of stone, I chucked them toward the opening and Eli hauled them away.

Hannah leaned into the new doorway. "The access is adequate now. Cedric, are you ready?"

"Ready for what?" My gaze shot to Cedric. "And how are we going to revive her?" I asked. My granddaughter Zoe had thinned and grayed after being buried ten years, but she hadn't dehydrated to the point of shriveling. Not much anyway. I'd given her an IV and used my powers to heal her. Why hadn't I thought to bring food or medical supplies? How would I get anything into Rebecca if I could barely touch her?

"That's my job. Joseph, Kayla, I'm ready for those

blood bags," Cedric called out, then snatched a knife from his pocket. He knelt over the lifeless form, leaning close to her mouth, then he sliced across his hand. He curled his fingers to control the flow as blood streamed from his vein and into Rebecca's mouth. Moments later, his hand healed and he cut it again.

Ouch. He would definitely need those blood bags.

"Kayla, while you're at it, would you throw us one of those blankets, please? Rebecca will need to be covered up soon." I sprinted over to the hatch and glanced up to see Joseph. He tossed me a clump of blood bags and then the blanket floated down. "Thank you," I said as I caught everything.

After returning to Rebecca's tomb, I laid the blood bags on the floor. Knowing we didn't want anything rubbing against her just yet, I set the blanket aside.

I wanted to help but I didn't know where to begin. How effective would my healing powers be on someone who was nearly dead? But I had to try, because Cedric's energy was already waning. He'd given too much. "Why don't you take a break and recharge? I'll see what I can do until you're full speed again."

"You're right. This could take a while and I need to be able to go the distance." He set the knife down, his wrist already healed, and went for the blood bags.

I kneeled next to Rebecca. My hands hovered a couple inches above her, and I mentally connected with her. Though I couldn't pick up any images, the energy in her body seemed stronger. I closed my eyes to concentrate, summoning all my healing essence, and pushed it into her.

I envisioned her organs reforming, her veins plumping, her muscles swelling, her brain tissue reconnecting and her heart pumping blood.

"Wow."

I jolted at Cedric's voice, my eyes opening and cutting to him. Oh, no, what now?

Chapter Five

I WAS WEAK, and my vision blurred from exerting so much energy to heal my mother. "What's wrong?"

"Nothing at all. Look at her." He pointed at Rebecca.

I rubbed my eyes to remove the fuzzy vision. Though Rebecca still appeared small and dry, she'd filled out, become more solid. "That was fast."

"Fast?" One eyebrow rose. "You've been at it for two hours. I've been watching and marveling at your ability, but I was starting to worry about you. I'll take over while you eat."

Eat what? I didn't smell anything. I flattened my palm on the stone floor to balance myself while I stretched my legs. But my knee gave out and I teetered to the side.

"Easy." Cedric caught me, hooking a hand under my arm and lifting me up until I was standing. He shifted, his hand sliding around me until I leaned against his side. Such proximity to him made me dizzier and I swayed again. He steered me to the pile of rocks we'd removed from the wall and eased me to them. He bent in front of me, his hands on my thighs. "Are you okay?"

"Just a little drained, I guess." I peered over his shoulder. "Did you say food is around somewhere?"

He grinned. "I wouldn't call it food, not exactly. But it'll provide energy."

Just when I thought he expected me to drink blood—not appetizing whether human or vampire blood—he dipped into his jacket pocket and offered me a protein bar. "Eat. I'll resume feeding her while you recharge."

A protein bar was better than nothing and I devoured it gratefully. Hannah, Eli and Charlotte had disappeared. "Did the others leave?"

"Yes, but they're coming back with real food. Should be back any time. And then they're leaving again. Joseph will go with them to make room for Rebecca in our car and Kayla will stay."

I bit off a chunk of the bar, doubting it had much protein. Tasted more like a sugar bar. But sugar would give me energy so I didn't care. While I chewed, I surveyed the tomb, but my eyes drifted back to Rebecca. "Do you think the blanket will bother her?"

"No. If she's not cold already, she'll feel it soon." Instead of cutting his hand again, Cedric located the blanket nearby and spread it over her. Then he returned to feeding Rebecca.

"Thank you." My balance and strength were already improving. As I finished the last of the protein bar, I shuffled around the dark, dank dungeon. Under the entrance hatch, I glanced up. With the dilapidated ladder, how would we get Rebecca out? Maybe the ladder could take my weight, but it certainly couldn't handle an additional person at the same time.

I swiveled around and studied Cedric as blood dripped from his hand and into her mouth. He'd already given so much and a part of me expected him to solve this last problem for me too. But that wasn't me. I'd been on my own since I was sixteen. I didn't need a man to bail me out of difficulties. I glanced up at the hatch again. It was about eight feet up and about four feet wide. If I jumped with the extra weight of my mother, I risked not making my target. I wouldn't want to hurt her.

The warmth of Cedric's body heated my skin and I turned to find him just inches away. I'd been too engrossed in figuring out how to get Rebecca to the car that I hadn't heard him move.

"Hey, you're worrying too much. I can get her out. I'm an ancient vampire, remember? I can jump that, even with the extra weight of Rebecca."

"Safely?"

"Yes, I promise," he said softly, rubbing my arm. "Trust me."

His thumb skated across my skin, sending shivers through me. Why did he have to be so compassionate and tough at the same time? That was a heady mixture, and a lot for me to resist. "I'll try to relax. Thank you."

The scent of food reached my nose and I glanced at the opening above. "We should take a break and have a real meal. Besides, she's already started the healing process and we've both given her enough fuel to continue repairing even if neither of us is with her."

Cedric waved to the exit. "After you."

"Coming up," I called out, then climbed the old ladder. The scent of food hit me harder, but I calmly stepped out of Cedric's way and waited for him. An instant later, he was right behind me, his palm on my lower back. Lord, he needed to stop touching me so much.

Why were his hands always making contact with me? My stomach fluttered at the idea that Cedric might actually be interested in me as more than just a friend. But I was getting ahead of myself. The only thing I should be focusing on at the moment was getting Rebecca healed enough that we could move her. And then getting home to my people. I had responsibilities, serious ones, and had no business fantasizing about a man with whom I had no future.

Cedric handed me a foil tray. "Hope Mexican food is okay."

"Only psychos don't like Mexican food." I grinned and rested my bottom against the edge of a boulder.

"C'mon." He jerked his head toward the Bentley where Kayla had opened the hatch and lowered the tailgate. He held my food while I hopped up, then I held his blood bag. "Taking off now?" he asked Charlotte, Joseph, Hannah and Eli.

I set down my bowl and hopped to the ground, then hugged each one of them. "Thank you so much for all your help. And for the food."

"Not a problem. Never a bad idea to have a powerful witch on our side. Or two of them." Joseph winked and headed toward the car.

"That's not why we did it." Hannah rolled her eyes.

"Let me know when you're on your way to the castle and I'll tell Autumn to make sure your mother has a quiet room waiting for her."

After another round of hugs and some tears on my part, they drove away.

"I'm going to patrol the area again," Kayla announced before leaving Cedric and me alone.

We sat side-by-side in silence while I finished my meal and he sipped on a blood bag. When I had eaten every last morsel, I shoved my empty tray into the paper bag and sighed. "That was amazing."

"I avoid human food since it can weaken us, but sometimes I make an exception for Mexican. I should take you to my favorite restaurant near my home. You'll die when you taste their enchiladas." He squeezed out the last of the blood from the bag and peered over at me when I didn't reply.

In an effort to avoid any awkwardness, I blurted out the first thing that came to my mind. "That sounds great."

He dropped the blood bag into the paper bag, then shoved it in a corner in the back of the SUV. "It's a date."

I blinked, wondering how I had allowed myself to walk into that one. A date that would lead to what? Both of us alienating our own people? "We should check on Rebecca." I made a beeline for the hatch and dropped down.

Cedric landed behind me an instant later, zoomed past me, then spun around and blocked my path. "Do I make you uncomfortable?"

I swallowed. Being thrown into difficult circumstances and not knowing what to say, I found honesty was always the best policy. And if I couldn't be honest and real with my friends, were they really true friends? "Sometimes."

Cedric tilted his head. "Why?"

"Because," my gaze darted around the dungeon, "sometimes I'm not sure of your intentions. And then I'm not sure how to react."

He nodded, studying me. "Allow me to make things more clear." Then he stepped closer until we were a foot apart. "You intrigued me from the moment I saw you on Hollywood Boulevard over fifty years ago. I was drawn to you, but you were very young. I wanted to do the honorable thing and let you grow up. So I gave you plenty of time to live your life and experience the ups and downs, and learn from them." Cedric closed the distance and his mouth was just inches from mine. "You've had your chance to do those things. Now I want *my* chance."

Apparently, Cedric's philosophy to fall back on honesty matched mine. I hadn't imagined, for even an instant, that he might return my feelings. But he did. The man I'd fallen for decades ago wanted me!

But just because he returned my feelings didn't mean all our barriers fell away. Perhaps I had been better off not knowing how he felt about me. Sure, he wanted his chance, but what did that really mean? Oh, why was I entertaining this right now? I already knew it could never work between us and I had other things to concentrate on, like bringing a witch back to life.

"Well." I took a step back. "You've certainly given me something to think about."

As I brushed past him, his hand slipped down my arm, his fingers entwining with mine, then he pulled me against him. "You can add this to your list of things to mull over."

Cedric leaned in and I didn't move a muscle. I'd been dying to kiss him since that day in the ice cream shop. Stopping him now never crossed my mind. I even angled my head as soon as his lips touched mine, giving him access to deepen the kiss. And he did.

Chapter Six

FIRE BLAZED THROUGH my body and I reeled from the blast of sensation of his mouth on mine. I gathered the fabric of his shirt and balled it in my hands, dragging him closer. I wanted more.

What was I doing? Considering the time we'd spent together, we barely knew each other. It would take time to see if we could commit to the long haul. Except that I lived in Scottsdale, a six-hour drive from his home in Calabasas, California. Did he even have the patience for a long-distance romance? Or did he believe I would drop everything so he could continue being king?

But he'd already told me Dathan planned to take over. I had my doubts Dathan would follow through. From what I'd heard about him, he didn't like being tied down. Even if he did reclaim the throne, I still had my people to protect and I couldn't imagine any of them welcoming a vampire into their fold.

I released my grip on his shirt and stepped away. "Y-you took me by surprise."

Cedric chuckled. "Kind of surprised myself too.

Eavesdropper Kayla from above just told me to give you space, at least allow you the chance to revive your mother before I swoop."

"We don't know for sure she's my mother." But I'd bet anything she was.

"Divine witches were thought to be extinct. From what I've gathered, especially considering how difficult she was to kill, Rebecca is most likely a divine witch. You've never met your mother, but you didn't magically materialize from thin air. The date Mortimer entered in his journal when he doomed Rebecca to eternity in a tomb matches around the time you were a baby and motherless. Chances of her not being your mother are slim, I think."

"When you put it that way." I should have said something more intelligent, something worthy of coming from a queen's mouth. But I was still breathless from his kiss. The kiss I shouldn't be thinking about. "Let's check on my mother."

Still a little disoriented after Cedric's confession and still lightheaded from the kiss, I darted over to my mother. The shape had grown and filled out more. I dropped down beside her, my pulse leaping. "She doesn't look so shrunken now. When do you think she'll become conscious again?"

Cedric shrugged, kneeling beside me. "Could be anytime. My gut is telling me we should wait to move her though, let her heal more. We don't want to risk hurting her."

And that meant more time with Cedric. Alone. Except for Kayla above ground who could hear us. But I didn't really care if Kayla heard everything. I just wanted to kiss Cedric again.

"Hey." His palm brushed between my shoulder blades, sending a delicious shiver up and down my spine. "I'm sorry about earlier. That was inappropriate and extremely poor timing."

Was he already regretting it? "Not a problem. Although, to be honest, I feel a bit scattered, like I need to be concentrating on her and not my personal life."

"Then we'd better carry on." He brandished his dagger, then cut his palm and curled his fingers to let the blood flow into my mother's mouth.

Now that her flesh had become more solid, and I wouldn't accidentally take a chunk out of her, I laid my hands on her stomach for direct contact so I could get closer to her insides. More direct energy could mean a faster recovery. I closed my eyes, sending my healing energy through her.

Every part of my body targeted hers, and all my mental energy focused on her cells, organs, bones, muscle tissue and her brain. I imagined her organs growing, her heart beating and blood flowing through her veins to every cell throughout her body. I imagined impulses firing through her brain, and waking her up.

Cedric's arm whipped around my waist, catching me as I tipped over. "We need to get you more food."

I shook my head as I struggled for balance, and glanced up at him. "How long was I in a trance this time?"

"An hour and a half maybe." He nodded toward Rebecca. "Wow, she looks just like you."

I sucked in air when I saw her. No longer a shriveled, dried out mummy, and though she appeared to be a very old woman, her face had grown rounder. Her body had filled out too, her arms less bony.

"Can we move her now?"

"I believe so," Cedric answered as he carefully scooped the fragile body into his arms. He swiveled to face me and beamed. "I can't wait to officially meet your mother."

"You and me both." I rearranged the blanket around her, tucking it in where I could. I didn't want her getting cold out there. "I still can't believe we found her. When she wakes up, what will I say to her?"

Images flooded my mind—a blond woman holding an even blonder baby dressed in pink. And then another image of her, seeing me as I'm being taken away. She had overheard Cedric and she knew who I was. I bit my bottom lip to keep it from trembling.

"Wait." I clamped onto Cedric's arm so he wouldn't leave just yet. "She's awake and communicating with me." I laid a hand on her and choked on a sob. "You're safe now. Save your strength so you can heal quickly."

"Kayla, I'm coming up with Rebecca. Stand by to take her." Cedric bent his knees a moment, then shot straight up into the air with his burden. As soon as he cleared the hatch, Kayla snatched Rebecca and Cedric landed. He gained footing, then they all disappeared out of my view.

I gathered up the protein bar wrapper, all our tools and flashlights, then sprinted up the ladder. The sun winked from the horizon. It would be light soon.

Kayla accessed the car hatch to get another blanket, then opened the door to spread it over the backseat. Cedric rounded the hood to the door, leaned over the backseat and arranged Rebecca so she would be comfortable.

"Jane, get in on the other side," Kayla said. "She can use your lap as a pillow."

"Quickly. It's getting light," Cedric urged. "After being in the dark for decades, the sun will be cruel on her eyes."

With my mother's head on my lap, I stroked her blond hair. Dirt stuck to my fingers and my heart ached for her. First thing I'd do when we got back—after she was strong enough—I'd run her a hot luxurious bath.

I pressed my fingertips against her chest to detect her heartbeat. My eyes pooled when I felt the movement. Wheezing of her lungs told me she was breathing now.

"You guys must be hungry again," Kayla tossed over her shoulder from the driver's seat. "Let's get something in the next town."

An image of a hamburger invaded my head and I chuckled. "I don't think you're going to be able to eat for a while. But I promise, as soon as you're able to move around, I'll take you out for a burger. In the meantime, you shouldn't use your energy sending me images. You need to save that for healing."

She still hadn't opened her eyes—they probably hadn't fully hydrated yet—but I knew she was awake. "While we're driving, I'll tell you about the new world you've woken up to. It's been over seventy years since Mortimer locked you away."

)

Once I settled Rebecca into the guest room, I covered her with a clean blanket and turned her over on her other side for a change of pace. I busied myself with little tasks, like gently brushing her hair, carefully covering her skin with lotion and whatever else I could think of to make her more comfortable. And, of course, I periodically used my healing powers on her.

But it had been hours and hours. She hadn't woken again and I was restless. I rose to take a stroll around the castle and stretch my legs.

"Water," she whispered. "Please."

My heart skipped a beat and I brushed the back of her hand with my fingertips. "Okay. I'll be back in a few."

As I left her room into the adjoining sitting room, Cedric rose from the chair. "How is she?"

I grinned. "Thirsty. I've been sent for water."

He returned my smile, and fell into step beside me. "That's a good sign. It means her body is winding down on the big repairs and is now fine-tuning the healing process."

"And as she hydrates, I'm sure talking will get easier."

Cedric opened the door for me that led to the hallway. "Most of the food and energy goes toward healing the bigger more important things. The body addresses small flaws and wrinkles later. Could be a while before she looks as young as you, but she'll get there."

We arrived at the kitchen and I opened cabinets for a pitcher or something to hold water. "Can I get you something?" a brunette werewolf asked.

"A big container of water for my patient," I replied, ready to take it back to my mother. "I think she'll need a straw too."

She bowed, then quickly located a pitcher. Instead of handing it to me, she placed it under a water spout. "I'll bring it to your mother's room shortly, Your Majesty." The werewolf offered me a warm smile.

After being totally engrossed in finding my mother, then watching over her in an unfamiliar place, I'd forgotten I was a queen and a guest of the werewolf palace. I could ask a servant for things like food and water. That would certainly make caring for my mother easier. "Great. Thank you so much."

"Our cue to get out of her kitchen." Cedric chuckled, his hand finding my hip and steering me back into the corridor.

"What brings you by?" I asked. I hadn't seen Cedric since we'd brought my mother in hours ago. He had coordinating to do with Dathan and preparations for the summit, so I understood why I hadn't seen him. Despite caring for my mother being a full-time job and keeping my mind occupied, I found I actually missed Cedric.

"Just checking up on you two. Mind if I visit your mother and see for myself?"

"Please do." I pushed open the door to the guest room in time to see her trying to get out of bed. I rushed over and blocked her, raising her legs and placing them back on the bed. "What are you doing?"

Her eyes narrowed. "As grateful as I am for being rescued," she whispered in a hoarse voice, "I can't stay in this bed forever."

"You're supposed to be healing." I remained in her path. She needed to save her strength, not exert herself.

"Which I've been doing since you found me last night." Her eyes lit up when the servant entered with the tray of glasses and a pitcher full of water. "Thank you," my mother rasped, grabbing the glass and chugging as the werewolf bowed and slipped out.

When she'd downed the entire cup, I refilled it with the full pitcher. "You can barely talk. You need to save your energy."

"Who is this?" Rebecca aimed a look at Cedric. "Wait. You're a vampire. You were the one who saved me?"

Cedric shook his head. "Not exactly. It was a group effort. All of us helped."

Rebecca reached out a hand toward Cedric and he crowded next to me to accept it. "But you gave your blood to heal me. You carried me out. Thank you," she whispered. Already I could hear her voice getting stronger as the water rehydrated her throat.

"No worries. I'm glad to see you doing better. I'll leave you two alone." Cedric backed out and disappeared.

"Mom, I need you to stay in bed. Please," I pleaded when she tried to swing her legs over again. "We'll be traveling in just a few days and you need to be strong enough."

She leaned back on the pillow, tears welling in her eyes. "Mom. I never thought I'd hear you say that word. Didn't think I'd ever see you again." She hugged me when I bent closer, anchoring her arms around my neck. When the hug-fest waned and I withdrew, she gripped my hand. "King Mortimer?"

"Dead. The werewolves are under kinder management now. In fact, you're their guest." I drank in her lovely face. "But we need to travel back to the witch's castle, about eleven hours from here by car."

"The witch's castle?" She shook her head. "That didn't go well last time. I ended up running for my life, only to be captured by wolves. Who is their ruler now?"

"Actually..." So much had changed since my mother had been taken prisoner, tortured and killed. "Me."

Her eyebrows rose. "You're the witch queen?" she asked, choking on a sob.

"Yes." I chewed my bottom lip a moment, wondering if I should fill her in more slowly. Oh, to hell with it. "And... I have three granddaughters who'll be thrilled to meet you."

"Granddaughters?" She covered her face and wept, tiny little muffled sobs filling the room. A knock on the door had my mother wiping the tears from her cheeks.

Autumn popped her head through the opening. "Am I interrupting anything?"

My mother waved her in. "Come on in."

"Mom, this is Queen Autumn, the one who slew Mortimer," I said, offering my chair to Autumn. "The new werewolf king, her husband Zack, found the tunnels and Autumn came across Mortimer's journals. When she read an entry about you, she called me right away."

"I don't know how I can ever repay you," my mother whispered.

"You already did." Autumn said, leaning over to bow. "Without the help of your witches, we couldn't have won the battle against Mortimer. My kind will be forever grateful to you, Queen *Jane* and the others."

My mother's eyes cut to mine. "Queen *Jane*? That's you?"

"Yes," I answered. "I wasn't sure of my real name, so I went with Jane Doe."

Rebecca huffed. "Jade is your given name. I hope you don't mind if I call you that."

I grinned. "I wouldn't mind at all." I would probably change my title officially at some point. But for now, it didn't matter. At least I knew Jade was my real name. And now I knew my real mother.

"Well, I just wanted to pop in and say hello. I hope you'll let me know if you need anything." Autumn shifted to me. "Since everyone is here, I thought we could have the summit earlier, like in a couple of hours. Dathan and Natasha are anxious to get started on their honeymoon. And I'm guessing you're anxious to get the summit out of the way so you can concentrate on your mother. What do you think?"

"Sounds wonderful." The sooner the summit ended, the sooner I could get my mother home. I couldn't hold back the grin at the thought of her reaction when she met her great-grandchildren.

Autumn shot me a warning look. "You're not traveling alone again, I forbid it. I'll send some guards with you. If you're driving, you can take the Land Rover and my guards will drive it back."

"Thank you so much for everything." I would have preferred Cedric escort us, but he'd already gone out of his way for me.

"My pleasure. Now I have to go do queen stuff." Autumn winked and slipped out the door.

"So we're friends with vampires *and* werewolves? There goes the neighborhood." Her voice sounded better and she no longer needed to whisper. In her shoes, I'd be dying to get out and walk around.

I laughed. "You sound good. I think I'm okay with you walking around, but only a little bit. How about a hot bath?"

She shuddered in pleasure. "Yes, please."

"And tomorrow, we'll go out, see how the world has changed. Perhaps buy you some clothes."

"Yes, but at some point soon, I need to earn my keep." She gave me a stern look. "And don't get used to mothering me. I'm the mom. I'll be ordering you around soon enough."

My eyes misted, loving her view and loving that I finally had my mother. I'd waited long enough. "Don't worry. I won't forget."

Chapter Seven

I PARTICIPATED IN the summit that evening while my mother bathed, then watched TV wide-eyed, learning a little more about the new world before seeing it in real life. The summit ran smoothly and I added my signature to the treaty signed by Dathan, Cedric, the shape-shifter queen Natasha, Zack and Autumn.

The next morning, I took my mother shopping for clothes. Although Cedric had business to attend to, he sent Kayla and Joseph to watch over us. We followed my mother into every store she had a whim to browse. She couldn't get enough of the shops, the people, the fashions, and everything else that was so different than when she'd last seen it. One of her stops was in a luggage store so she could transport all her belongings.

By the end of the day, I never wanted to see another mall for the rest of my life and we returned to the werewolf palace. Having not totally healed, my mother was pretty wrecked and I felt awful for letting her exhaust herself which could set her healing back.

"I'll handle the bags. I don't want you overdoing

it anymore than you already have." I shooed her away from the car trunk.

"I'll get some of them." Kayla snickered. "I'm sure you can carry them on your own but I don't think you'll get through the doorway."

Joseph reached into the back of the car. "I'll get the suitcases." Kayla and Joseph delivered the packages and bags to my mother's room, then slipped out.

"Sit. I'll put your things away." As I began transferring the contents of her bags into the dresser drawers, she eyed me from the bed. "What?" I asked.

"Cedric," she said, barely above a whisper. "What are you going to do about him?"

I shook my head, really not wanting to get into that with her or anyone else. I plucked a blouse from a bag and hung it on a hanger. "Absolutely nothing."

"Hm."

I inwardly rolled my eyes, wanting to stop her in her tracks if she planned any kind of matchmaking. "I've been figuring out my life just fine for decades. I'm hoping you're not going to tell me who I should be with or try to run my life."

Her face fell and she lowered her gaze. "I overstepped. I'm sorry."

Uttering one syllable was hardly overstepping. I spun and groaned. "No, I'm the one who should be sorry. It's just that..." I blew a delicate raspberry, then schooled myself to speak quietly so Cedric wouldn't overhear. "I've always had a thing for him. But I can't see myself having a real relationship with a vampire.

And we each have our own kingdoms to rule." Cedric may have a reprieve coming up, but eventually Dathan would tire of being king and Cedric would step in, just as he always did.

She covered my hand in hers. "When we want something bad enough, we don't see obstacles. We get so intent on accomplishing our goal, the roadblocks just vanish. But when we know someone is wrong for us, we come up with all kinds of reasons why. Maybe he's just not for you."

Cedric sure felt right for me and I definitely wanted him badly enough—even more so after that fiery kiss in the tomb. "Protecting my people is my number one priority. I could never choose a man over the witches I've sworn to lead and protect."

"You can't have both?" my mom asked, pushing a pile of underclothes at me to set into a drawer.

"Apparently not." I wasn't going there with her or anyone else. Time to switch the subject. "The peace summit is over and you've healed enough to travel. We should leave first thing in the morning."

"How far away is your palace?" she asked, tucking her knees up under her chin.

"A one-hour flight if it's nonstop." I grunted and sagged, then grabbed another bag of clothes to put away. "Even if I could get another ticket for you on that same flight, you don't have identification or anything that proves who you are. We'll have to drive."

My mother lit up at the light knock on the door. "Come in."

The werewolf servant entered holding a tray with two small plates, each with what looked like chocolate lava cake. I'd learned earlier that her name was Sarah. "Her Majesty requested I bring you refreshments."

My mother's eyes widened. "Yes, please."

Sarah giggled and set the tray on the night stand. Then she handed us each a plate and spoon. She curtsied and slipped out of the room.

I swallowed a bite, then returned to my task, carefully folding a T-shirt and laying it in the drawer. "We could get a rental, but Autumn offered one of her cars, along with guards. That'll take eleven hours, longer if we linger at each stop."

"Part of me doesn't want to rush the trip. I could stay here, finish healing and watch TV." She gave me a wistful smile. "But I don't want to wait to meet my great-granddaughters."

"Then it's decided." My heart ached at having to leave Cedric. But I wouldn't desert my people anymore than I could desert my granddaughters. And now my mother. I couldn't just invite Cedric to the witches' palace and then shack up with him there. What kind of an example would that send my granddaughters when I barely knew him?

I glanced at the drawers I had just filled with all her new clothes. I'd have to transfer everything to the suitcases, but the evening was still young and packing would give me something to do while we chatted.

"I've been wondering..." My mother paused, another forkful of lava cake at her lips. "What happened to their mother, your daughter?"

"She's alive." My gaze fell to the bed my mother sat on and I sighed. "She never embraced being a witch, so her magic is dormant. When she thought she lost Zoe, she just kind of gave up, which ruined any chance I had of making her realize she had powers. She granted Tessa custody of Bree and they came to live with me."

My mother cocked her head. "Do you see her much?"

"She thinks Zoe and I are dead. But we keep tabs on her from afar. Would you like to come with me next time I check in on her?"

My mother beamed and nodded. "That would be lovely."

Clearly, she was anxious to see all her relatives. I didn't want her waiting any longer than necessary. "If we're leaving in the morning, we should say goodbye to our hosts soon." I'd have to say goodbye to Cedric. Again. My heart sank.

)

I'd said goodbye to almost everyone, including Sarah the sweet brunette who had helped me in the kitchen and served us lava cake. But not Cedric. I tracked him down to the newly landscaped gardens at the other end of a long row of roses. I snuck up behind him, even though I knew he'd catch my scent.

"Hi." I gave him a hesitant smile when he finally circled to face me.

"I hear you're leaving shortly." Cedric's eye twitched. "Even though you originally planned to be here four more days."

"My mother is anxious to meet and get to know her great-granddaughters, which is totally understandable." I licked my lips, wondering if he was angry with me. Would he miss me? The thought of leaving Cedric filled me with sadness. But I couldn't very well invite myself to Cedric's castle and he needed to return home anyway, at least until Dathan and Natasha came back from their honeymoon.

What if I invited him to the witch's palace and he stayed a while, then decided he didn't want me? I couldn't afford to give my heart to any man and have it broken.

"I see." Cedric's face lost all expression. "I gave you space, time to grow, and you only slipped further away. I guess it wasn't meant to be."

I couldn't face him and the sadness in his eyes. When my gaze dropped to the floor, he took that as my reply. "Please wish your mother well for me." And then he was gone.

A hollowness radiated through my chest.

Chapter Eight

WE SPENT TWO days on our road trip because my mother wanted to stop and drink in every small town— and nearly every big one. Since Autumn's guards assured me they loved road trips and were in no hurry to get back to the werewolf castle, I let my mom do whatever she pleased. Finally, we arrived in Scottsdale. I invited the werewolves to stay and recharge, but they insisted on not imposing on us. They left almost as soon as they delivered us to my home. My mother received a warm and surprised welcome home, blending right into the family.

She healed more over the days, her skin hydrating and repairing. She appeared to be in her fifties now, which was about the right age to be my mother, since I looked like I was in my early thirties. Eventually, she would look my age but until then, her being great-grandmother to Tessa, Zoe and Bree was slightly more believable.

Two weeks later, I was in my office catching up on work, struggling not to think about Cedric, and that rejecting him could've been the biggest mistake of my life. What if I never met someone like him again? What if I lived all eternity alone?

But I couldn't take that mental path. I could only consider what was best for my people and my family.

My mother poked her head into the office. "Do you have a few minutes?"

I smiled. "Of course. Come on in. I was just wrapping up before breaking for lunch." I slid my paperwork aside and waved her to the leather chair on the other side of my desk.

"You've raised some lovely girls." My mother glowed with love.

"I didn't really raise any of them. I was gone for a few years while I built my empire and they thought I was dead." I tapped my foot, instinct telling me that my mother wanted to say something more. Probably about Cedric, and that subject wasn't up for debate. "I've been meaning to ask you why you're so normal after being trapped for seventy years. Zoe was buried alive for a decade and spent five years getting her bearings. Why hasn't the time in the tomb affected you?"

"I never endured it." Her expression grew somber and she frowned. "I don't understand why I didn't die when he tried to kill me. I was mutilated, but for some reason that I still don't understand, I survived. But having no way for my body to function and no means to heal it, I never regained consciousness. Last thing I remember is being tortured by Mortimer's men and him commanding them to make sure they killed me this time."

I sighed, grateful she didn't have to suffer through what Zoe endured. And did my mother really not know she was a divine witch and couldn't be killed so easily? I unlocked my desk drawer and pulled out an ancient book, opening it to the page I had bookmarked years ago. I flipped the volume around and slid it across the desk. "You should read this section. It will explain why you survived that."

I watched as her expression ran the full spectrum of emotions, first shock and finally happy tears.

"I had no idea." She blinked as the information settled in her mind. "I knew I was different, stronger than other witches. But once I was running for my life, I didn't have anyone to talk to. I'm grateful to have that now."

I smiled. "We're all very fortunate."

"Yes, we are." She tapped her fingernails on my desk, her eyes narrowing. "You, especially."

I couldn't shake the feeling that she was hinting at something and I was probably being set up. "How so?"

She leaned back in the chair and crossed her legs, a smugness about her. "You could've ended up with a beautiful man who loves and adores you, who would've treated you like the queen you are. You had the chance at a lifetime of happiness with a wonderful and loving partner. Good thing you dodged that bullet, right? I hate to think what life would have been like if you'd fallen into that trap."

And there it was. Apparently, she was going to make up for all the mothering she'd missed these past decades. I groaned. "Mom, I can't choose him over my species."

"You know you wouldn't have to." She leaned forward, resting her chin in her palm. "I watched him watch you, and I saw the way you looked at him. That man would've done anything for you, would've followed you anywhere. Don't throw him away because you're scared. You have to at least try."

I grunted. "Actually, I don't."

"Don't act like a five-year-old, darling. Be a grown-up. Be brave. Risk it all for someone who would give his life for you. Love recklessly. But most importantly, go and get that man. Fight for your happiness. If you don't, no one else will."

My mother would fight for my happiness, obviously. But I didn't want to encourage her so I didn't say that out loud. Instead, I rolled my eyes. "Even if I wanted to forget my pride and chase after some guy who I'd spent a whole five minutes with, I don't know where to find him and I no longer have his number. Even if I tracked him down, he's probably already moved on."

Not that I would even consider crawling back to Cedric when he couldn't possibly still want me after the way I had abandoned him. I just wanted this conversation to end.

"But if you don't try, you'll never know. Someday, you're going to regret pushing him away. The girls were fine when you were gone. They can handle your kingdom for a while. And I'll be able to help them. If they have any questions, they can always call you." My mother, the busybody, rose from the chair then leaned over to slide a half sheet of paper toward me. Then she strode out of the room.

I hoped she wouldn't bring up Cedric again. Relief filled me at the idea of being off the hook, at least for now. I glanced down at the piece of paper with Cedric's name... and an address and phone number.

Damn. My mother had waltzed in and filled me with hope, then given me a way to make my wish come true. Maybe Cedric wasn't the one. Or maybe he was. I'd already been without him for over fifty years and I didn't want to wonder for the next fifty years if it could've worked out.

Mostly, I just missed Cedric.

I raced to my room, grabbed my luggage and went through my closet. Tessa and my mother appeared in the doorway. "You leave now and you can go shopping when you get to his castle," my mother said.

"Seriously, Grandma, you need some new clothes anyway." Tessa sighed. "You haven't treated yourself in ages."

She was right. I hadn't taken time out for myself in months and I couldn't remember the last time I'd bought new clothes. I simply hadn't had the time. But I had plenty of help now. "You're handling the money now, Tessa," I threw over my shoulder and smirked. "Make sure to transfer some into my spending account."

"We're going with you so we can make sure you're safe." Zoe grinned as she tugged on Chait's hand. "You can just drop us off at Magic Mountain and we'll find a room at a nearby hotel. We're due for a vacation anyway. If that's okay with you."

I squinted, wondering who masterminded their scheme. "Fine. I'm leaving in five minutes, with or without you two."

Zoe's boyfriend Chait slung an arm around her waist. "We've been packed all day. The Expedition is already gassed up and ready to go."

I fisted my hands on my hips. "This was a total setup."

"Of course it was." My mother crossed the distance and hugged me. "Because we love you. And after all these years of self-sacrifice and devotion to others, you deserve happiness of your own."

My eyes stung and I cleared my throat to wash away the urge to weep. "Thank you, all of you. Now, get out of my room so I can gather up a few things. I can't arrive looking wilted and worn."

I shooed them out, then threw my makeup bag, hair stuff and several of my favorite pairs of shoes in my suitcase, along with a handful of outfits to hold me over until I went shopping. Just before I headed out of my room, I paused. If things didn't go well with Cedric, what would I do? Maybe I'd go somewhere far away and hide out for a while to lick my wounds. I rummaged in my desk drawer for my passport and slipped it into my purse, then raced down the hallway to find Chait and Zoe waiting for me in the foyer.

Butterflies fluttered in my belly. I was really going to do this.

Chapter Nine

WHEN I DROPPED off Chait and Zoe at the hotel where they had reserved a room, the sun had already been hidden for a couple of hours. I hoped Cedric didn't have plans to go out for the evening.

I had called Dathan during one of our stops under the pretense of apologizing for leaving so soon after their wedding. My real reason for talking to him was to make sure Cedric was at the vampire palace, as the address on the piece of paper had indicated. "Have you already taken over for Cedric?"

He laughed once. "I've been brought up to speed and ready for days. But I can't get rid of him. He keeps coming up with things to do and reasons not to leave."

If he couldn't drag himself away from work for himself, why would he do it for me? He talked big about leaving his kingdom behind and exploring the world, but in the end, he couldn't do it. I would never be more important than his people.

As it should be. But I was already twenty minutes from the vampire palace. I'd come too far—over four hundred miles—to throw in the towel now.

The map took me to a secluded and exclusive neighborhood with tree-lined streets, luscious lawns and gorgeous blooms. Long stretches between mansions gave me too much time to stress and my clammy hands kept sticking to the steering wheel. I patted my palms on my black slacks and willed myself to be calm.

When I pulled into the driveway, a security gate stopped me. The button and speaker meant I had to identify myself. There went my surprise entrance. Cedric would be warned of my arrival. Would he even consent to see me? Would he send me away? Or would he just quietly slip out the back to avoid me?

I rolled my window down and pressed the button.

"Can I help you?" a woman asked from the speaker.

I was in luck. "Kayla, is that you? It's Queen Jane. I was hoping to surprise Cedric. Will you let me in?"

Did Kayla just snort? I couldn't make out the muffled noises but a moment later, she cleared her throat. "I won't say a word to him. Pull up close to the front door and I'll make sure it's unlocked. Just come right in. I'll meet you at the door and take you up."

Okay...

I did as Kayla directed, leaving my belongings in the trunk, then I let myself in through the front door. She waited for me in the foyer, an index finger vertical across her lips. Then she motioned for me to follow. In silence, I shadowed her up the stairs and down the hallway.

I know you can't speak telepathically, but you can hear me, right? she asked and I nodded. *I'll give you access into his suite, and then you're on your own. Okay?*

No, not okay at all! What if he met me with fury? Or worse, boredom?

I nodded again. She stopped at a door, punched in a code, then pushed it open. After a quick tap on the doorframe to warn Cedric, she nudged me forward.

Here I go. My stomach twisted.

"Who is it?" Cedric rumbled from another room.

He sounded grumpy. Oh, just great. I took a deep breath and crossed the threshold but he was nowhere to be seen. Across the sitting area of his suite, an open door came into view and I crept toward it.

"Who's there?" Cedric called out.

"Me."

In an instant, he stood in front of me, his eyes guarded. "What are you doing here?"

That was a very good question. Cedric was clearly moody and not overjoyed to see me. But I'd made the trip for a reason and I didn't want to spend the next thousand years regretting all the things I hadn't done.

"Well..." I swallowed, gripping the car keys still in my hand. Oh, geez, what should I say? Seconds ticked by and I panicked. He probably thought me such a fool. But one important thing I'd learned through my life was that people responded to honesty and they sensed when someone was being genuine. I would just speak from the heart. Since I didn't have Cedric anyway, I didn't have anything to lose.

"I'm such an idiot and I shouldn't have let you go without telling you how I feel about you." There, I'd said it. I just wished my voice didn't squeak while the words passed through my lips. "Whatever is happening between us, I want to see where it leads."

His face lit up. "Took you long enough," he growled, then he descended, snagging me around the waist with one arm and the other hand cradling my neck, the sheer pressure lifting me off the ground to bring me eye-level with him. He crushed me so hard against him that I couldn't breathe and then his mouth devoured mine, taking away the last of my breath.

I hadn't been held or kissed like that by a man in forever. When his tongue grazed mine and tingles overtook my body, I became absolutely positive I'd *never* been kissed properly—until Cedric came along. When he released me and I slid down his chest, my brain had already stopped functioning. Cedric had kissed me stupid.

"What do you think about Paris for a first date?"

My brain reengaged and I slid my arms around his neck. "I'll go anywhere with you."

He kept me close against him and dropped a kiss on my forehead, then my eyelid and down to my temple. "When do you have to be back?"

"I left my mother in charge and she has Tessa to help. If they need me, they have my number."

He rested his forehead against mine. "I thought I lost you. You can't know what that did to me, what went through my head."

"A little grumpy, were you?" I couldn't help the smug grin sneaking onto my face.

"Worse than that." He laughed. "I can only imagine the relief that Kayla and the others will experience once I'm gone."

That would explain her reaction when I'd identified myself at the gate and her eagerness to personally escort me to Cedric's suite.

A calm settled over me, wiping away any apprehension or stress, and I couldn't find any part of me that had any doubts about running away with Cedric. My joy was probably coming out through the stupid grin on my face. I didn't care what Cedric thought—because I didn't need to worry anymore. I finally, truly, understood how he felt about me—exactly how I'd felt about him since our long chat in the soda shop decades ago. "The sooner we leave, the happier they'll be. It just so happens, I have a passport in my purse and my bags are already packed."

"I'll file flight plans immediately. Just one thing before we go." He gently brushed a few strands of hair off my face. "You should know, now that I have you, I'm not letting you go again."

I stretched up and kissed his scruffy ginger chin. "I'm depending on exactly that."

The End

)

If you enjoyed this book, please recommend it to friends, reader's groups and discussion boards or tell others how much you enjoyed it by reviewing it on Amazon, GoodReads or your own site.
Thank you and happy reading!

SHAPES OF AUTUMN SERIES

Thrown to the Wolves:
The Legend of Hannah & Eli
(prequel)

My Wolf's Bane (book one)

Wolves at the Door
(book two)

Dead Wolf Walking
(book three)

The Dark Wolf (book four)

Lord of the Wolves (book five)

Different species. Mortal enemies. It'll never work, but they'll die trying.

More Titles by Veronica Blade

A newbie witch enlists help from the scrumptious school bad-boy to make her life and death choice between two battling covens.

The witch queen must make the impossible choice between abandoning the throne and her people, or spending eternity with the man she loves.

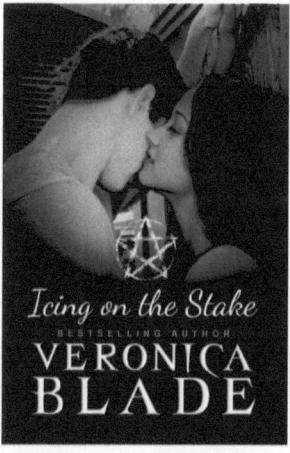

Sofia lays her hard-won anonymity on the line by saving the most popular boy in school. Worse, she's been exposed to the vampire hunters who attacked him.

A Cinderella who spends her nights as a wolf. A prince with a taste for blood.

More Titles by Veronica Blade

Should a woman who's unable to forget her first love give "happily ever after" one more try?

When good-girl Maddie switches places with her famous bad-girl twin Jackie, she has some pretty high stilettos to fill.

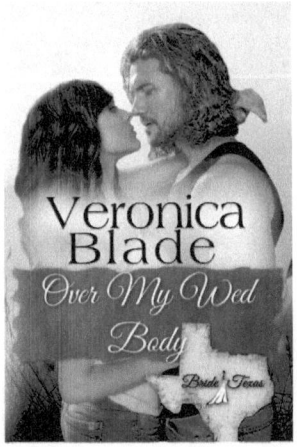

When Hunter realizes he botched the annulment of his marriage to his longtime friend, he must decide if she and their marriage are worth fighting for.

A micro trilogy including Single-Handed, Singled Out (book two) & Single-minded (book three).

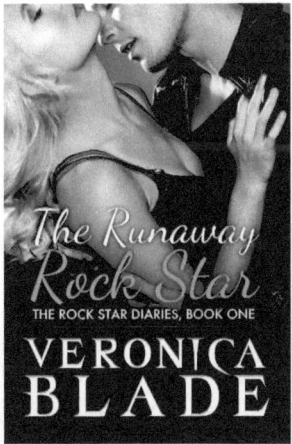

About Veronica Blade

Veronica Blade lives near Carson City, Nevada with her husband and furbabies but also spends a lot of time in southern California. She writes sweet romances to live vicariously through her characters. Except her heroes and heroines lead far more interesting lives—and they are always way hotter.

)

You can visit Veronica Blade on Facebook, check out her website or follow her on Twitter. You can even e-mail her at veronica@veronicablade.com. She loves hearing from readers!

www.ingramcontent.com/pod-product-compliance
Lightning Source LLC
Chambersburg PA
CBHW020636130626
46552CB00003B/1252